Hot Winter Nights

MELODY RAINNE

Hot Winter Nights

Melody Rainne

Also By Melody Rainne

Tell Me You're Mine

One

I'M DATING THE GRINCH. Seriously. He may not be all green and fuzzy, but still. To be honest, I think the man hates Christmas more than the actual Grinch does. Which totally sucks for me because I absolutely love Christmas. It's my favorite time of the year. I wouldn't say I'm obsessed, but it's slowly creeping towards that point. Well, it is if you ask Jack.

Jack Porter and I have been together for about five years now. I always knew that he didn't like Christmas, but I hadn't realized just how much until recently. At first it didn't really bother me, but this year I've had enough of being in love with a Grinch. Something had to change.

This year I planned to change his mind. I was

willing to do whatever it took to make him believe in Christmas again.

I was in love at the most magical time of the year, and I wanted it to be just as magical for him, Grinch or not.

He has been away for work for a couple weeks now so I wanted to do something really special for him. Both as a welcome home and to show him how amazing Christmas truly can be.

I spent many hours running from store to store searching for the perfect decorations. For my plan to work I had to make the house look as festive as possible. Since Jack was away I left all my purchases laid out all over the living room so I could keep a quick inventory of what I already had. It took several trips, and much more money that I had anticipated, but once I was done and everything was all set up, I'm sure it would be more than worth it.

I grabbed my checklist I had made and went over it a couple times, making extra sure I wasn't missing anything. Satisfied I had it all, I set it aside and looked around at the current red, green, and silver mess currently taking over my living room. There was a lot of stuff here, I realized. Like, a lot. I was really glad Jack wasn't here right now to see this. I'm sure he would have something to say about all the money I spent. But

I didn't care. It was my money after all, and I was making some Christmas magic here.

I grabbed my coat to make what I hoped would be my last run out to the store for a while. I would be needing a few more plastic totes to be able to store all the decorations after the holidays. I checked my watch. Crap. I was cutting it close. I drove to the closest store and grabbed all the totes I could carry.

Back at home I quickly stored the totes in the spare room and put up the decorations in record time. The tree was put up, fluffed, and decorated. Garland was hung on the staircase, mantle, and all the doorways. Twinkle lights filled the rooms with a magical glow. I didn't trust myself with real ones, so there were battery operated candles on the mantle as well as each table and counter. They were red, green, and silver and covered in sparkles. What's Christmas without sparkles everywhere?

I hung the new matching stockings I bought over the fire, and put up the wooden santa's sleigh with his reindeer that my grandfather had carved many years ago. It was one of my favorite decorations. I made sure to put it up every year, even if it was the only thing I did put up.

I had a few houses I had slowly collected over the years. I took those and some fake snow and turned one of the corners of our living room into a cute little snowy village.

I stepped back to admire my work. It looked like I lived inside a Christmas store. I loved it. Hopefully it would melt Jack's Grinchy heart.

I still had just enough time to bake the cookies and make the hot cocoa that I wanted to. I thought it would be a nice treat for when he got home. Nothing was better than a hot mug of cocoa after spending some time out in the cold snow. And it sure was coming down today. I really hope Jack doesn't have any trouble making it home okay.

I threw the cookies in the oven and started heating the pot on the stove for the cocoa. Then I ran upstairs to put on my special outfit for welcoming home my man. Well, the first of two. I was going all out this year.

Since I would be finishing up the baking as he came home, outfit number one was very simple. It consisted of bright red lipstick, a cute tie-on apron, a Santa hat, stilettos, and . . . nothing else. It was bold, I have never worn anything like this before. But I was feeling a little frisky, and really hoped it would help change his mind about hating Christmas.

Checking myself out one more time in the mirror, I was satisfied Jack wouldn't be able to resist. I made my way back downstairs. From the smell of things the cookies were coming along nicely.

I could feel the excitement bubbling up inside me. It's been such a long time since I've done any sort of surprise for Jack. And this is the first time I've done a sexy surprise. Along with the excitement were waves of nervousness.

I couldn't wait for him to come home.

Two

I MUST HAVE TEXTED Jack a hundred times asking him his location and what time he thought he would be home. I wanted everything to be absolutely perfect.

The snow was now coming down pretty hard. I checked the fire in the fireplace, adding a couple more logs to it. I knew Jack would appreciate the warmth. While the snow was beautiful to look at, it sucks to have to be out and about in. Especially if you have to drive anywhere. Winter driving absolutely terrifies me. Whenever Jack was home he would volunteer to do most of the driving for me. It was one of the many reasons I really hated the fact that he had to travel so much for his job. Other than the fact that I missed him like crazy whenever he was gone. Five years together and I still felt like a lovesick teenager around him.

The timer on the stove beeped, letting me know that the cookies were finished baking. I made two different types - soft ginger cookies and brown sugar spiced shortbread. As soon as I opened the oven door the house was filled with the warm scent of cinnamon. I breathed in the scent. It was comforting. And it was one of the scents that always reminded me of the holidays. My mom would always bake the same two types of cookies every year. The smell of them baking felt like home to me.

After setting the cookies on the cooling rack, I gave the hot cocoa a stir. It smelled heavenly. It was the perfect thing to warm him up after being out in the cold.

I could hear the sounds of the snow crunching under car tires, meaning Jack was home. It was showtime!

I quickly put a couple cookies on a small plate and filled a festive mug with delicious cocoa. I then set both on one of our small wooden serving trays. Grabbing the tray, I quickly made my way to the front door, being careful not to spill any of the treats.

When Jack opened the door he was greeted to the

sight of me holding the tray, wearing practically nothing. To say he looked shocked was an understatement.

The way he looked at me still, after all these years, it was just about enough to bring me to my knees. The fact that he still wanted me after all this time, meant the world to me. He meant the world to me. I want to do everything I can to show him just how much he does mean to me. How much I love and appreciate him.

Jack dropped his stuff off by the door, never taking eyes off me. It made my heart flutter. "What's all this?" he asked, taking in the sight.

I set the tray down on the coffee table and turned around in a slow circle. "Merry Christmas," I said. "I missed you."

"I, uh . . . I missed you too," he said, staring at my lack of clothing.

"You like it?" I asked, heat creeping up to my face. Before I was feeling all confident and sexy. But standing here in the living room wearing practically nothing was starting to feel a little awkward. I don't normally walk around the house naked or anything. But judging by the look on his face, maybe I should do it more often.

"Oh, I like," he growled.

And before I knew it his mouth was on mine. Jack

grabbed my waist, pulling me into him. I wrapped my arms around him, as he kissed me like it was the last time he'd ever be able to.

I laughed as I jumped into his arms, wrapping my legs around his hard, muscular body. This man was mine. He slowly made his way upstairs to our bedroom, kicking the door open and throwing me on the bed. He quickly undid his tie and unbuttoned his shirt, throwing them both on the floor.

He crawled on top of me, with a look in his eyes that said he couldn't wait to devour me. That look alone sent shivers throughout my body.

"Leave it on," he instructed as I reached to untie my apron. I obeyed, reaching out instead to grab Jack and pull him down to me. The second his lips met mine, electricity raced through me. This man turned me on like no other.

He deepened the kiss, grabbing a fistful of my hair. Arching my back, I could feel how much he wanted me. I reached down, running my hand along his erection, which was fighting hard against the constraints of his dress pants. With a little fumbling, I managed to unbutton his pants, freeing him.

"On your back," I whispered, nipping at his ear. I slid his pants all the way off, tossing them on the floor. Turning my attention back to him, I crawled over, taking him in my hands. With one hand I slowly pumped up and down on his shaft, while I bent down and ran my tongue over the tip.

"Jesus, Scarlette," he breathed. Jack laid his head back, eyes closed. I took the full length of him in my mouth, slowly grazing my teeth over the shaft as I moved up and down. Jack started to thrust his hips in response. I don't know how it was possible, but Jack got even harder.

I alternated between sucking on the tip and taking him all the way to the back of my throat until he stopped me. I looked up at him, biting my bottom lip. "Something wrong?" I ask.

"God no," he said breathlessly. "I just need you, now. I need to be inside you," he said as he flipped me around. He wasted no time as he lined himself up with my entrance and with one thrust, buried himself inside me. I gasped as he filled me, over and over again. I felt how much he wanted me, how much he needed me. And I needed him just as much.

With each thrust, I felt us getting closer and closer. Not only to an orgasm, but to each other. Jack was mine. He was home. I've never loved anyone the way I love him. There was nothing needy or possessive. There was just an undeniable bond, a deep, passionate love that just seemed to grow over time. I don't know what I would do without this man. He was my whole world.

And right now he was rocking it.

Jack quickened his pace and we moved together, our bodies becoming one. His body went rigid against mine and I pulsed around him as we both found our release. I cried out his name as I clung to him, holding him close.

Panting, he collapsed in my arms. "I love you," he whispered into the crook of my neck.

"I love you too, Jack."

We both lay there in each other's arms, not wanting to move as we caught our breath. "I missed this," I said, nuzzling into him. He was warm, he was safe. He was home.

"Me or the sex?" he asked with a laugh.

"Both, but mostly just you." I kissed his cheek. He had the right amount of stubble. "You work too damn much." He really did. Lately he seemed to be at work more than he was at home. And then there was all the added traveling he had to do. I hated it. I absolutely hated it. But I sure did love our reunions.

Three

"YOU REALLY WANT me to wear this?" Jack asked, holding the red fuzzy boxers up in front of him.

"Of course," I shrugged. "I mean, I'd prefer you to be completely naked, but it's a little too cold for that."

"I'm still going to be cold."

"I lit a fire," I pointed out. "Oh, don't forget about the bow tie."

He picked it up, balancing it on one finger. He took one look at it and laughed, shaking his head.

"What?" I asked innocently. "It completes the outfit."

"If you say so," he shook his head again. "And I'm not really sure you can call this an outfit." I turned to look at him. Holy hell was my man sexy. He stood there, in nothing more than red fuzzy boxers, a red bowtie, and a matching santa hat. I just wanted to run my hands up and down his rock hard abs, leaving a trail of kisses all down his body.

My outfit matched his. I wore red fuzzy panties, a matching bra, and the same Santa hat he wore. Not your typical Christmas outfits, but it was exactly what I had in mind. I wanted to show him that Christmas can be both fun and sexy. That it wasn't a bad thing, and that he should stop being such a Grinch.

I took out my phone and snapped a few pics of us, promising Jack that no one but the two of us would ever see them. This was something I definitely wanted to remember.

After posing for way too many pictures we went downstairs for the cocoa and cookies that we had previously abandoned.

"So what is all this for?" Jack asked around a mouthful of cookies, gesturing both to our outfits and the many, many decorations placed all over the house.

I couldn't tell if his tone was upset or anything. What if he hated it? "You don't like it?" I asked, sticking out my bottom lip in a fake pout.

He set down his cookie, and moved to take me in his arms. "That's not what I meant, babe. I love it. I just meant that I hadn't expected this. We never decorate for the holidays." Or celebrate at all, really.

"That's exactly why I did it," I tilted my head back to look him in his eyes. "Because we never celebrate. Because you hate Christmas."

"I don't hate Christmas," he argued.

"Liar. Like you said, we've never decorated, we've never really even celebrated. We've never done any of those things, you've never even bought me a Christmas gift. Not that a gift was expected or anything, it was just part of the experience. Besides," I said, planting a kiss on his chin, "you are my gift."

Jack rolled his eyes at that. "You're so cheesy."

"Maybe, but it's true." Standing on my toes, I pressed a quick kiss to his lips. "And you love me for it."

"That, I do," he looked down at me with those lustful eyes. Taking his right hand and cupping my face, he trailed his thumb across my bottom lip. My lips parted, letting out a small gasp. Even the smallest touch from him turned me on.

"Is that what I think it is?" he asked, nodding up at the ceiling fan. I had hung a sprig of mistletoe on each of the fan blades. And in each doorway.

"Mmmm, it might be," I said playfully.

Smiling devilishly, he grabbed my head in his hands. "You know, if this is what Christmas is like every year with you, I think I could get used to it," he said.

"Oh yeah?"

"Definitely," he said before crushing his mouth to mine.

Four

ALMOST THE EXACT second his lips touched mine, all the lights went out. "Wow," I laughed. "That was one powerful kiss."

"You should know by now just how powerful my love for you is," he growled, which went straight between my thighs. The things this man could do to me without even touching me.

The power seemed to be out in the entire neighborhood. The snowstorm was so bad it took out some power lines. Luckily I had lit a fire and set out the flameless candles everywhere. It was actually more romantic this way.

Jack and I grabbed a bottle of wine and two glasses and settled down on the carpet in front of the fire. I watched him as he carefully poured us both a glass.

Shadows danced across his face from the flames. The warm glow made him look sexier than he's ever been. I don't know if it was purely from the fire, or because I was so turned on, or even if it was a little Christmas magic, but this moment right here, it was absolutely perfect. I have never wanted Jack more than I do right now. I knew there was nothing that could ever tear us apart.

Grinch or not, he was my man.

Maybe we really didn't need all the fancy decorations or gifts or holiday cheer. Just being here with him, lying in his arms by the fire as the storm raged on outside, was more than enough for me. His love was all I needed.

"Do you really think I'm the Grinch?" he asked, stroking his hand up and down my arm. It sent shivers up my spine.

I laid my head on his shoulder, cuddling him close. "I used to," I laughed. "But this right here is absolutely perfect."

Jack kissed the top of my head. "I'm so glad you think so. But," he said, taking my wine glass and setting them both on the table beside us. "I think I have something that will make this moment even better."

He moved to face me, sort of on one knee. Staring

into my eyes, he slowly slid one hand down into the front of his boxers.

Oh, I liked where this was going.

But instead of doing what I thought he was doing, he pulled out a small box.

"Jack," I breathed.

"I love you so much. I'm sorry I've been away for work for so long. And I'm also sorry that I've been a Grinch," he laughed. "I told my boss that this last work trip was it, that I wasn't doing it anymore."

My heart skipped. "Seriously?" I could feel the tears prick at the back of my eyes. Do I really get to spend every day and night with him? I really no longer have to say goodbye as he left me alone for up to a couple weeks at a time?

"Seriously. I know how hard it's been on you with me away all the time. And I, too, miss you like crazy. I can't stand being away from you. And I don't want to spend another second without you. So Scarlette Reeves," he opened the box to reveal the biggest diamond I've ever seen, "will you marry me?"

"Oh Jack, of course I will," I cried. I threw myself into his arms.

Never in a million years did I imagine I would be proposed to by candlelight at Christmas time.

Best. Christmas. Ever.